W9-CPB-810

¿Qué tiempo hace? / What's the Weather Like?

Está nevando
It's Snowing

Celeste Bishop

traducido por / translated by

Charlotte Bockman

ilustrado por / illustrated by

Maria José Da Luz

S
xz
B

PowerKiDS press.

New York

Published in 2017 by The Rosen Publishing Group, Inc.
29 East 21st Street, New York, NY 10010

First Edition

Managing Editor: Nathalie Beullens-Maoui
Editor: Katie Kawa
Book Design: Michael Flynn
Spanish Translator: Charlotte Bockman
Illustrator: Maria José Da Luz

Cataloging-in-Publication Data

Names: Bishop, Celeste.
Title: It's snowing = Está nevando / Celeste Bishop.
Description: New York : Powerkids Press, 2016. | Series: What's the weather like? = ¿Qué tiempo hace? | In English and Spanish. | Includes index.
Identifiers: ISBN 9781499423136 (library bound)
Subjects: LCSH: Snow–Juvenile literature. | Weather–Juvenile literature.
Classification: LCC QC926.37 B57 2016 | DDC 551.57'84–dc23

Manufactured in the United States of America

CPSIA Compliance Information: Batch #BS16PK: For Further Information contact Rosen Publishing, New York, New York at 1-800-237-9932

Contenido

Contents

Grandes copos blancos caen del cielo.
¡Está nevando!

Big, white flakes are falling from the sky.
It's snowing!

La nieve es un tipo de clima.

Snow is a kind of weather.

La nieve viene de las nubes en el cielo.

Snow comes from clouds in the sky.

La nieve es una señal de que ha llegado el invierno.
Donde vive mi familia nieva mucho.

Snow is a sign winter is here.

It snows a lot where my family lives.

Los copos de nieve pueden ser grandes o pequeños.
Cada uno es diferente.

Snowflakes can be big or small. Each one is different.

¡Los atrapo con la lengua!

I catch them on my tongue!

Mi mamá dice que puedo
salir a jugar en la nieve.

My mom says I can go
play in the snow.

Hay que abrigarse.

It's time to get bundled up.

13

Me pongo mis botas y mi abrigo.

I put on my boots and coat.

Los guantes mantienen mis manos calientes.

Gloves keep my hands warm.

Mi hermana y yo hacemos un muñeco de nieve.
Le ponemos un sombrero y bufanda.

My sister and I build a snowman. He wears a hat
and a scarf.

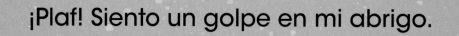

¡Plaf! Siento un golpe en mi abrigo.

Poof! Something hits my coat.

18

¡Es una pelea de nieve!

It's time for a snowball fight!

19

Mis amigos se deslizan en trineo colina abajo.

My friends are sledding down a hill.

Mi trineo va muy rápido.

My sled goes really fast.

Tengo frío cuando llego a casa.

I'm cold when I get home.

Un chocolate caliente me hará entrar en calor.
¡Delicioso!

Drinking hot chocolate will warm me up. Yum!

23

Palabras que debes aprender
Words to Know

(las) botas
boots

(la) bufanda
scarf

(un) copo de nieve
snowflake

Índice / Index